JE

LO

ACU
8010

SANTA CRUZ CITY-COUNTY LIBRARY SYSTEM

D0574588

JEASY

Reiser, Lynn.

Ten puppies /

2003. 2/04

DISCARDED

6/05-5(7/05)
4/08-15 (8/08)
LO 3/11

SANTA CRUZ PUBLIC LIBRARY
SANTA CRUZ, CALIFORNIA 95060

TEN
PUPPIES

Lynn Reiser

Greenwillow Books
An Imprint of HarperCollinsPublishers

This one is for Virginia

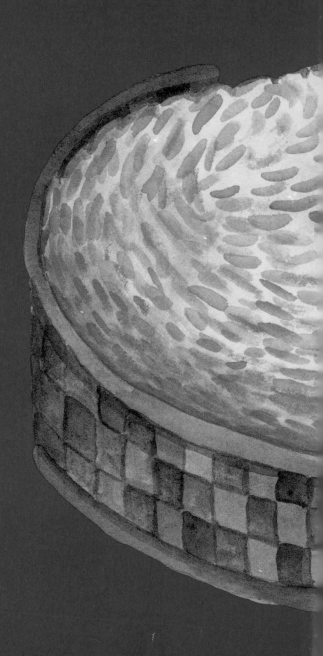

Ten Puppies
Copyright © 2003 by Lynn Whisnant Reiser
All rights reserved.
Manufactured in China.
www.harperchildrens.com

Watercolor paints were used
to prepare the full-color art.
The text type is Futura Book.

Library of Congress
Cataloging-in-Publication Data

Reiser, Lynn.
Ten puppies / by Lynn Reiser.
   p. cm.
"Greenwillow Books."
Summary: Puppies from one to ten are counted
and sorted according to their different features.
ISBN 0-06-008644-0 (trade)
ISBN 0-06-008645-9 (lib. bdg.)
[1. Dogs—Fiction. 2. Addition—Fiction.
3. Counting.] I. Title.
PZ7.R27745 Te 2003 [E]—dc21 2002023544

First Edition 10 9 8 7 6 5 4 3 2 1

 Greenwillow Books

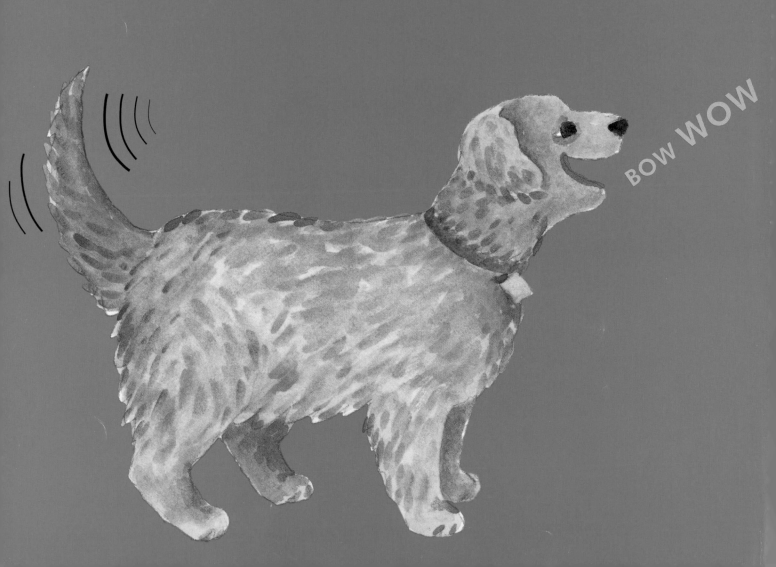

Puppy Rescue Center

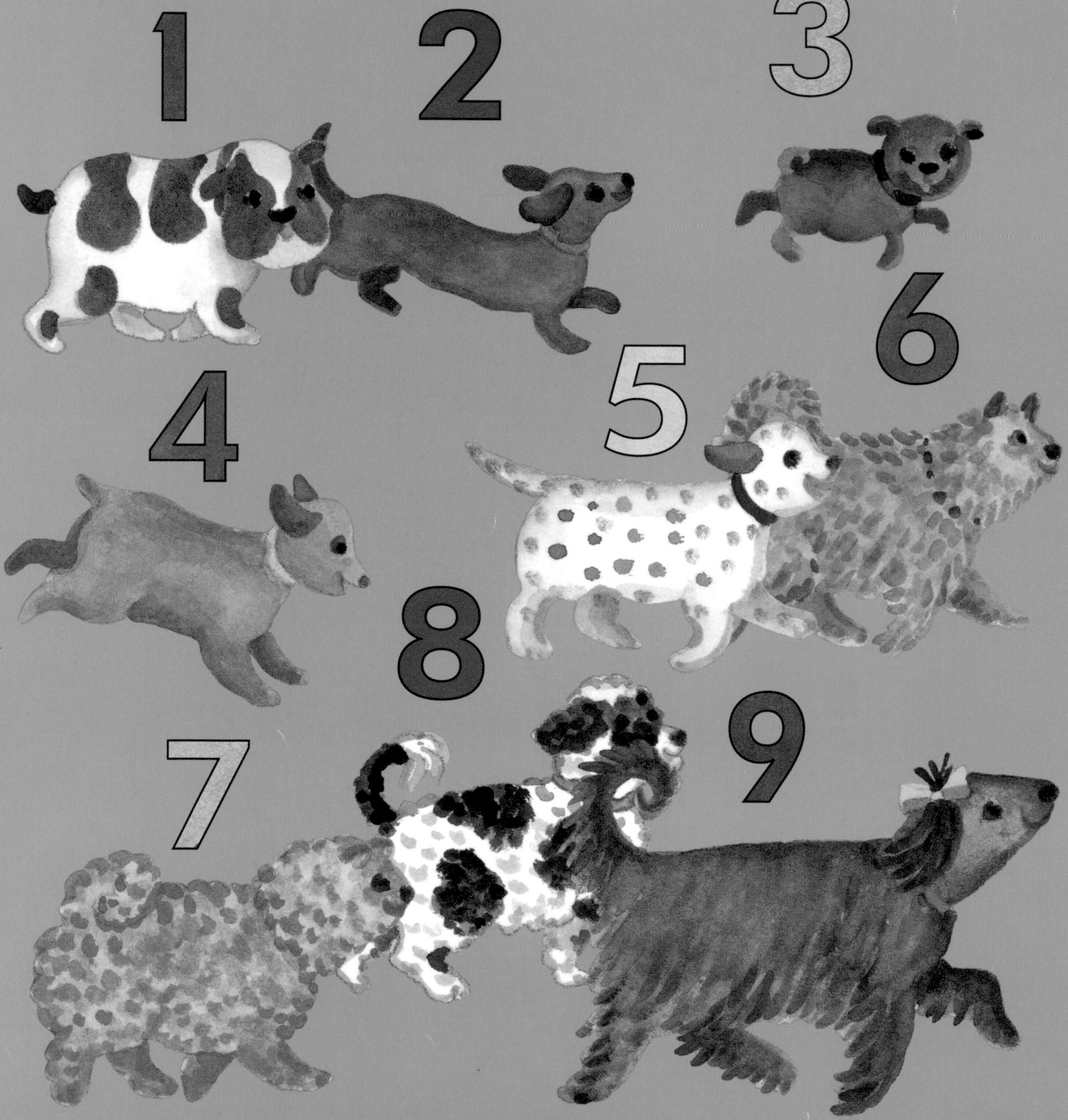
1
2
3
4
5
6
7
8
9

10

10

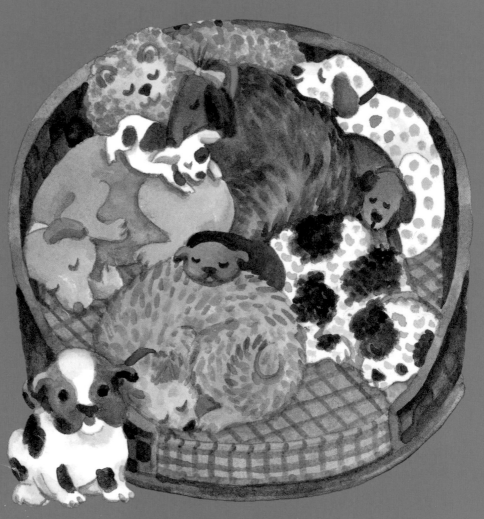

Mother Dog
raised TEN puppies.

9

NINE
had pink tongues.

1

ONE
had a blue tongue.

8

EIGHT
had pointed noses.

2

TWO
had flat noses.

7

SEVEN
had floppy ears.

3

THREE
had perky ears.

6

SIX
were plain.

4

FOUR
had spots.

5

FIVE
had curly tails.

5

FIVE
had straight tails.

4

FOUR
had shaggy fur.

6

SIX
had smooth fur.

3

THREE
had little paws.

7

SEVEN
had big paws.

2

TWO
had blue eyes.

EIGHT
had brown eyes.

1

ONE
was long.

9

NINE
were not.

Mother Dog
raised TEN puppies.

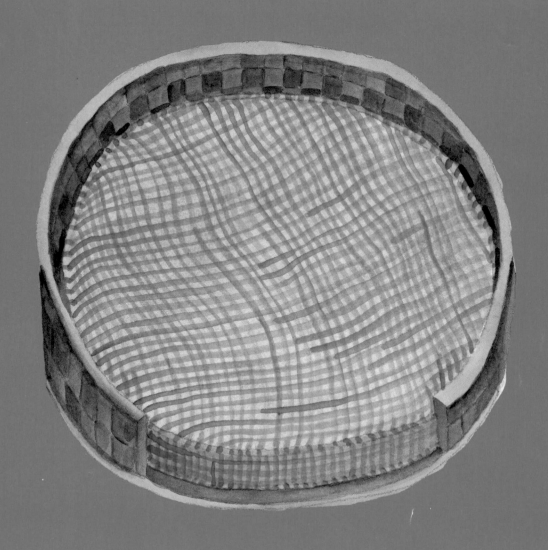

What did they grow up to be?

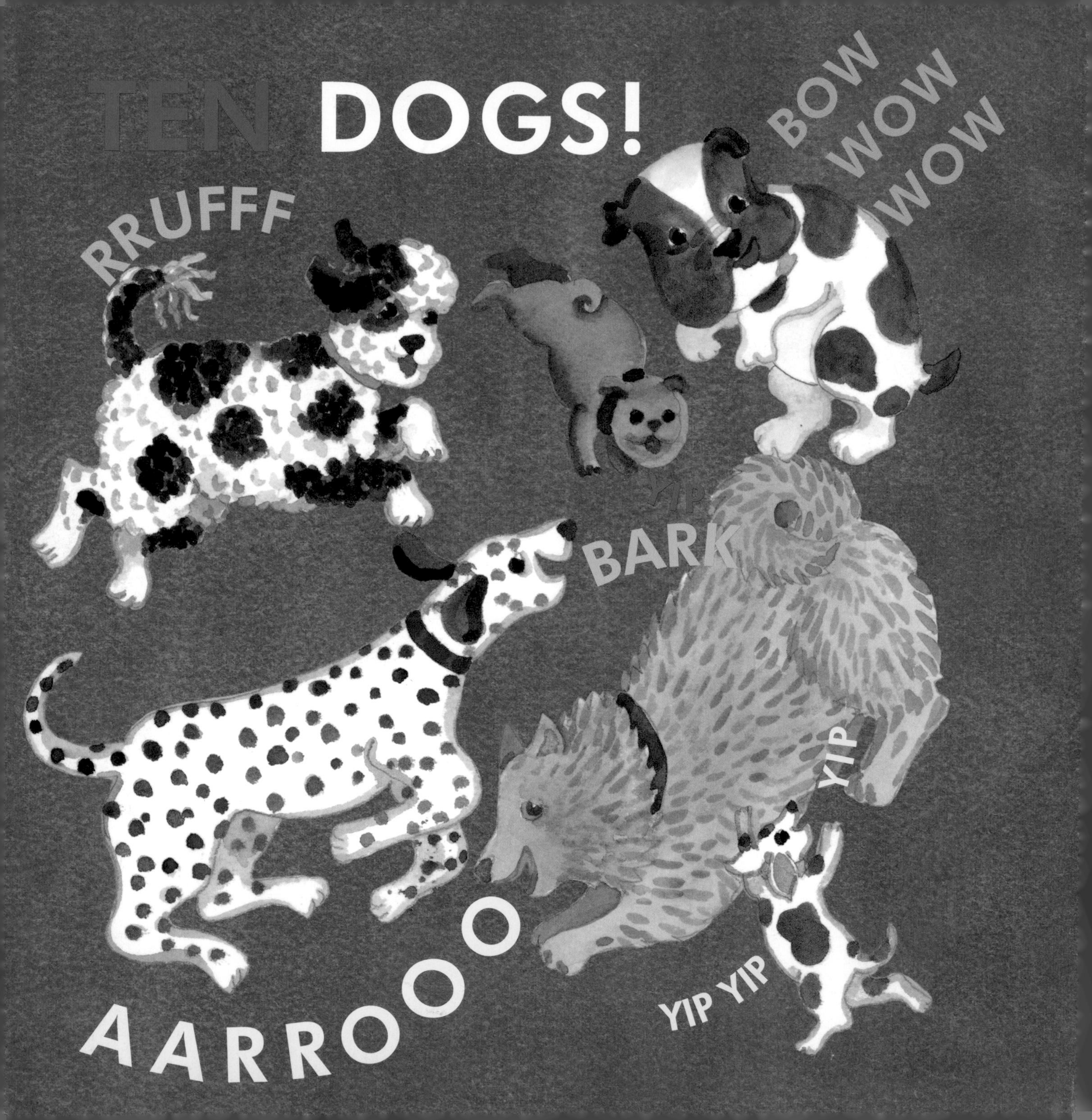

TEN DOGS!
BOW WOW WOW
RRUFFF
YIP
BARK
YIP YIP
YIP YIP
AARROOO

$9 + 1 = 10$

$1 + 9 = 10$

$8 + 2 = 10$

$2 + 8 = 10$

$7 + 3 = 10$

$3 + 7 = 10$

$6 + 4 = 10$

$4 + 6 = 10$

$5 + 5 = 10$

$5 + 5 = 10$